LITTLE HOUSE

Laura #10

Christmas Stories

ADAPTED FROM THE LITTLE HOUSE BOOKS BY

Laura Ingalls Wilder

ILLUSTRATED BY

Renée Graef

HarperTrophy ®
A Division of HarperCollinsPublishers

Adaptation by Heather Henson.

Illustrations for this book are inspired by the work of Garth Williams with his permission, which we gratefully acknowledge.

HarperCollins®, ☰®, Harper Trophy®, Little House®, and The Laura Years™ are trademarks of HarperCollins Publishers Inc.

Christmas Stories
Text adapted from *Little House in the Big Woods*, text copyright 1932, 1960, Little House Heritage Trust; *Little House on the Prairie*, text copyright 1935, 1963, Little House Heritage Trust; *On the Banks of Plum Creek*, text copyright 1937, 1965, Little House Heritage Trust; *By the Shores of Silver Lake*, text copyright 1939, 1967, Little House Heritage Trust.
Illustrations copyright © 1998 by Renée Graef
Copyright © 1998 by HarperCollins Publishers
Library of Congress Cataloging-in-Publication Data
Christmas stories : [adapted from the Little house books by Laura Ingalls
  Wilder] / illustrated by Renée Graef.
    p.   cm. — (A Little house chapter book)
  Summary: Laura Ingalls and her family celebrate several joyous Christmases
on the western frontier.
  ISBN 0-06-442081-7 (pbk.)
  1. Wilder, Laura Ingalls, 1867–1957—Juvenile fiction. [1. Wilder, Laura
Ingalls, 1867–1957—Fiction. 2. Christmas—Fiction. 3. Frontier and pioneer
life—Fiction.] I. Graef, Renée, ill. II. Series.
PZ7.C4539 1998   97-39293
[Fic]—dc21   CIP
                                                                         AC
First Harper Trophy edition, 1998

Visit us on the World Wide Web!
www.littlehousebooks.com

Contents

Contents

CHAPTER 1

Christmas in the Big Woods

Christmas was coming to the Big Woods of Wisconsin, where Laura lived with her Pa and Ma, her older sister Mary, and her baby sister Carrie. Their little log house was almost buried in snow. In the morning when Pa opened the door, there was a wall of snow as high as Laura's head.

The days were clear and bright, but it was too cold to play outside. Laura and Mary stood on chairs and looked out the window. Great big icicles hung from the roof of the little log house. The icicles were as fat as the top of Laura's arm. The sunlight made them shine like glass.

At the end of every day, Pa came in from the cold with white frost on his mustache and beard. He stamped the snow from his boots and caught Laura up in a bear's hug against his big, cold coat.

Every night, Pa was busy. He was making a Christmas present for Ma.

Pa took one big piece of wood and two small pieces and whittled them with his knife. He rubbed them with sandpaper and with the palm of his hand. When Laura touched them, they felt soft and smooth as silk.

Then Pa took his knife and carved beautiful shapes into the pieces of wood. He cut holes in the shapes of windows, little stars, moons, and circles. All around them he carved tiny leaves and flowers and birds. When he was finished carving, he put all the pieces of wood together.

Pa had made a shelf for Ma. He hung it carefully on the log wall between the two windows. Ma placed her little china woman on the shelf.

The little china woman had a china bonnet on her head. China curls hung against her china neck. She wore a pale-pink china apron over her china dress. And she wore little golden china shoes. She looked beautiful standing on the shelf Pa had made.

Every day, Ma was busy too. She was making good things to eat for Christmas. She baked bread and Swedish crackers. She cooked a huge pan of baked beans with salt pork and molasses. She made pies, and she filled a big jar with cookies. She let Laura and Mary lick the cake spoon.

One morning Ma boiled molasses and sugar together until they made a thick syrup. Pa brought in two pans of clean, white snow from outdoors. Laura and Mary each had a pan. Pa and Ma showed them how to pour the dark syrup in little streams onto the snow.

Laura and Mary made circles, and

curlicues, and squiggledy things with the dark syrup. The shapes became hard and were candy. Ma said that Laura and Mary could eat one piece each. The rest must be saved for Christmas.

Ma was doing all this cooking because Aunt Eliza and Uncle Peter and the cousins, Peter and Alice and Ella, were coming for Christmas.

Laura couldn't wait to see her cousins. She always played with Mary because Mary was her big sister and Carrie was too little to play with yet. And her cousins lived too far away to visit every day.

Laura liked playing with Mary most of the time. But Mary liked to play quiet games, and Laura liked to run and jump and shout. Laura's cousins liked to run and jump and shout too.

CHAPTER 2

The Cousins

The day before Christmas, the cousins arrived.

Laura and Mary heard sleigh bells ringing outside. The sound grew louder every minute. They looked out the window and saw a big bobsled come out of the woods and drive up to the gate.

Aunt Eliza and Uncle Peter and the cousins were in the bobsled, all covered up under blankets and robes and buffalo skins. They were wrapped in so many coats and shawls that they looked like big, shapeless bundles.

When they came inside, the little log house was full. The cat ran out and hid in the barn. Jack, the bulldog, leaped in circles through the snow. He barked and barked as though he would never stop. Now there were cousins to play with!

As soon as Aunt Eliza had unwrapped the cousins, Peter and Alice and Ella and Laura began to run and jump and shout all at once. Even Mary, who was always so good, couldn't help jumping and shouting too. At last Aunt Eliza told them to be quiet.

"I'll tell you what we can do," Alice said. "Let's make pictures."

Alice said they must go out in the snow to make pictures. Ma thought it was too cold for Laura to play outside. But when Ma saw how sad Laura was, she said she could go for a little while.

Ma put on Laura's coat and mittens

and the warm cape with the hood. Then she wrapped a scarf around Laura's neck.

When they were outside, Alice showed them what to do.

Alice climbed up on a tree stump. Then all at once she held her arms out wide and fell flat on her face into the soft, deep snow. Slowly and carefully she stood up and pointed to the ground. The shape in the snow looked exactly like a little girl. Laura

and Mary clapped their hands in delight.

All day they played at making snow pictures. Laura had never had so much fun.

They played so hard that when night came, they were too excited to sleep. But they had to sleep, or Santa Claus would not come. So they hung their stockings by the fireplace and said their prayers and went to bed.

Alice and Ella and Mary and Laura all slept in one big bed on the floor. Peter slept on the little trundle bed. Aunt Eliza and Uncle Peter were going to sleep in the big bed. Another bed was made on the attic floor for Pa and Ma.

The buffalo robes and all the blankets had been brought in from Uncle Peter's sled, so there were enough covers for everybody.

The little log house had never been so full. Laura and the cousins tried to fall asleep, but they could not. They were wide awake, listening to the grown-ups tell stories by the fire.

Finally, Ma said quietly, "Charles, those children never will get to sleep unless you play for them." So Pa got his fiddle.

The room was still and warm and full of firelight. Laura could see Ma's shadow and Aunt Eliza's and Uncle Peter's against the walls. Pa's fiddle sang merrily to itself.

Laura went to sleep listening to Pa and his fiddle sing softly.

CHAPTER 3

Christmas Morning

On Christmas morning, Laura, Mary, and all the cousins woke up at the same time. They looked at their stockings. Something was in them! Santa Claus had been there! Alice and Ella and Laura and Peter ran shouting to see what Santa Claus had brought.

In each stocking, there was a pair of bright-red mittens and a long stick of red-and-white-striped peppermint candy. They were all so happy, they could hardly talk. They just looked with shining eyes at their Christmas presents.

But Laura was happiest of all. Santa Claus had brought Laura a rag doll.

The doll was beautiful. She had a face of white cloth with black buttons for eyes. Her cheeks and mouth were rosy red, and her hair was black and curly. She had little red flannel stockings and little black cloth shoes. Her dress was a pretty pink-and-blue calico.

The doll was so beautiful that Laura could not say a word. She just held her tight and forgot everything else. She did not know that everyone was looking at her.

"Did you ever see such big eyes!" Aunt Eliza said.

The other girls were not jealous because Laura had mittens and candy *and* a doll. Laura was the littlest girl, except for baby Carrie and Aunt Eliza's baby. The

babies were too small for dolls. They were so small, they did not even know about Santa Claus. They just put their fingers in their mouths and wriggled because of all the excitement.

Laura sat down on the edge of the bed and held her doll. She loved her red mittens, and she loved the candy. But she loved her doll best of all. She named her Charlotte.

"Laura," Ma said gently, "aren't you going to let the other girls hold your doll?" Ma meant that little girls must not be selfish.

So Laura let Mary take the beautiful doll, and then Alice held her a minute, and then Ella. They smoothed the pretty dress. They looked at the red flannel stockings and the cloth shoes and the curly black woolen hair. But Laura was glad when Charlotte was finally safe in her arms again.

Then they all looked at each other's mittens and tried on their own. Peter bit a large piece out of his stick of candy, but Alice and Ella and Mary and Laura licked theirs to make them last longer.

Pa and Uncle Peter each had a pair of new, warm mittens. They were knit in little squares of red and white. Ma and Aunt Eliza had made them.

Aunt Eliza had brought Ma a large red apple stuck full of cloves. How good it smelled!

Ma gave Aunt Eliza a little needle book she had made from bits of silk and soft white flannel. The flannel would keep the needles from rusting.

They all looked at the beautiful shelf Pa had made for Ma. And Aunt Eliza said that Uncle Peter had made one for her with different carving.

Santa Claus had not given the grown-ups anything at all. It wasn't because they hadn't been good. Ma and Pa were good. It was because they were grown up, and grown-ups must give presents to each other.

Finally, all the presents were put away for a little while. Peter went out with the men to do the chores. Alice and Ella helped Aunt Eliza make the beds. Laura and Mary set the table, and Ma got breakfast.

For breakfast there were pancakes. Ma made a pancake man for each of the children. One by one, Ma called them to the stove so they could watch her make their pancake man.

Laura watched as Ma took a spoonful

of batter and put arms, legs, and a head on her pancake man. It was exciting to watch her quickly turn the whole little man over on the hot griddle. When the little man was done, Ma put it smoking hot on Laura's plate.

Peter ate the head off his man right away. But Alice and Ella and Mary and Laura ate theirs slowly in little bits. First they ate the arms, then the legs, and then the middle. They saved the head for last.

It was too cold to play outside. But there were the new mittens to admire and the candy to lick. They all sat on the floor together and looked at the pictures in the Bible. Then they looked at the pictures of all kinds of animals and birds in Pa's big green book. Laura kept Charlotte in her arms the whole time.

Soon it was time for Christmas dinner.

Now they could eat all the good things Ma had been cooking.

Laura and Mary and Peter and Alice and Ella had to sit quietly at the table. But they did not need to ask for second helpings. Ma and Aunt Eliza kept their plates full and let them eat as much as they could hold.

"Christmas comes but once a year," said Aunt Eliza.

As soon as they were done eating, Uncle Peter and Pa went to get the sled and horses ready. Aunt Eliza and Uncle Peter and the cousins couldn't stay any longer. They had a long way to go home through the snow.

Ma and Aunt Eliza bundled up the cousins. They pulled on heavy woolen stockings over their stockings and shoes. They put on mittens and coats and warm hoods. They wrapped scarves around their necks and put thick woolen shawls over their faces.

Ma slipped piping-hot baked potatoes into their pockets to keep their fingers warm. Aunt Eliza's flatirons were hot on the stove, ready to put at their feet in the sled. The blankets and the quilts and the buffalo robes had been warmed, too.

When they were as bundled up as they could be, they all got into the big bobsled. Pa tucked the last blanket around them. They looked cozy and warm.

"Good-by! Good-by!" they called, and off they went. The horses trotted through the snow, and the sleigh bells rang out in the frosty air.

In just a little while the merry sound of the bells was gone. Christmas was over. But what a happy Christmas it had been!

CHAPTER 4

Christmas on the Prairie

At Christmastime in the Big Woods, there had been lots of snow. But one Christmas there was no snow. Ma and Pa had taken Laura and Mary and baby Carrie and moved to a new little house far away on the Kansas prairie.

Winter days on the prairie were short and cold. The wind whistled and the hard rain fell. Day after day the rain kept falling. But still there was no snow.

Laura and Mary stayed inside, close

by the fire. They listened to the wind and the wet sound of rain as they sewed on their quilts and cut paper dolls from scraps of wrapping paper.

Every night was so cold, they thought for sure they would see snow in the morning. But in the morning they saw only sad, wet grass.

Laura was afraid that Santa Claus and his reindeer could not come without snow.

Mary was afraid that even if it snowed, Santa Claus would not be able to find them. They were so very far away on the prairie.

When they asked Ma, she said that she didn't know.

"What day is it?" Laura and Mary asked her over and over. "How many more days till Christmas?" Laura and Mary counted the days on their fingers until there was only one more day left.

Rain was still falling that morning. There was not one crack in the gray sky. They felt almost sure there would be no Christmas.

Still, Laura and Mary kept hoping.

Just before noon the light changed. The rain clouds broke and drifted apart. The sun came out and the birds sang. Drops of water sparkled on the grass.

Ma opened the door to let in the fresh, cold air, and they heard a loud roaring.

It was the creek!

Laura and Mary had forgotten about the creek outside their house. So much rain had made the creek wider and deeper. Now Laura and Mary knew they would have no Christmas. Santa Claus could not cross that roaring creek.

Pa came in bringing a big fat turkey. He said it weighed at least twenty pounds.

"How's that for a Christmas dinner?" he asked Laura. "Think you can manage one of those drumsticks?"

Laura said yes, but she didn't feel very happy.

Mary asked Pa about the creek. He said it was still rising.

Ma said it was too bad. She hated to think of Mr. Edwards eating his Christmas dinner all alone. Mr. Edwards was their neighbor. He didn't have a wife or a family of his own, so Ma and Pa had asked him to Christmas dinner.

"That current's too strong," Pa said. "We'll just have to make up our minds that Edwards won't be here tomorrow."

Of course that meant that Santa Claus could not come either.

Laura and Mary tried not to mind too much. They watched Ma get the wild turkey ready for Christmas dinner. It was a very fat turkey. Ma told them they were lucky little girls. They had a good house to live in, a warm fire to sit by, and a big turkey for their Christmas dinner.

Ma said it was too bad that Santa Claus couldn't come this year. But they were such good girls, and he hadn't forgotten them. He would surely come next year.

Laura and Mary knew Ma was right. Still, they were not happy.

After supper, they washed their hands and faces. They buttoned their red-flannel nightgowns and tied their nightcap strings. They said their prayers quietly and went to bed.

Pa and Ma sat by the fire. After a while, Ma asked Pa to play the fiddle.

"I don't seem to have the heart to, Caroline," he answered.

After a longer while, Ma suddenly stood up.

"I'm going to hang up your stockings, girls," she said. "Maybe something will happen."

Laura's heart jumped. But then she thought about the roaring creek, and she knew nothing could happen.

Ma took one of Mary's clean stockings

and one of Laura's. She hung them at the fireplace. Laura and Mary watched her over the edge of their bedcovers.

"Now go to sleep," Ma said, kissing them both good night. "Morning will come quicker if you're asleep."

Laura closed her eyes. Even with the stockings hanging at the fireplace, it did not seem like Christmas at all.

CHAPTER 5

Mr. Edwards Meets Santa Claus

On Christmas morning, Laura opened her eyes. She heard Jack growl, and then the door rattled.

"Ingalls! Ingalls!" someone said.

Pa opened the door.

"Great fishhooks, Edwards!" he cried. "Come in!"

Laura looked toward the fireplace and saw the stockings hanging limply.

She shut her eyes again. She heard Pa piling wood on the fire. Then she heard

Mr. Edwards say he had carried his clothes on his head when he swam the creek.

"It was too big a risk, Edwards," Pa said. "We're glad you're here, but that was too big a risk for a Christmas dinner."

"Your little ones had to have a Christmas," Mr. Edwards replied. "No creek could stop me after I met up with Santa Claus."

Laura sat straight up in bed. "You saw Santa Claus?" she shouted.

"I sure did," Mr. Edwards said.

"Where? When? What did he look like? What did he say? Did he really give you something for us?" Mary and Laura cried at the same time.

"Wait, wait a minute!" Mr. Edwards laughed.

Ma said she would put the presents in the stockings, as Santa Claus had intended. She said the girls mustn't look.

Mr. Edwards came and sat on the floor by their bed. He answered every question they asked him. Laura and Mary tried not to look at what Ma was doing.

Mr. Edwards told them how he was walking through town, when all of the sudden he saw Santa Claus coming down the street.

"In the daytime?" Laura asked. She didn't think anyone could see Santa Claus in the daytime.

"No," Mr. Edwards said. "It was night."

The first thing Santa Claus said was "Hello, Edwards!"

"Did he know you?" Mary asked.

"How did you know he was really Santa Claus?" Laura asked.

Mr. Edwards said that Santa Claus

knew everybody. And he knew Santa at once by his whiskers. Santa Claus had the longest, thickest, whitest set of whiskers west of the Mississippi.

"Edwards," Santa Claus said, "I understand you're living down by that roaring creek. Do you happen to know two little girls named Mary and Laura down there?"

"I surely do know them," Mr. Edwards replied.

"It rests heavy on my mind," said Santa Claus. "They are both of them such sweet, pretty, good little things, and I know they are expecting me. I surely do hate to disappoint two good little girls like them. But with the water up the way it is, I can't make it across that creek."

Santa Claus tugged on his whiskers and looked at Mr. Edwards with a twinkle in his eye. "Edwards," he said, "you look like you could make it across that creek. Would you do me a favor and take Laura and Mary their gifts this one time?"

"I'll do that, and with pleasure," Mr. Edwards told him.

Then Santa Claus and Mr. Edwards stepped across the street to the hitching post where Santa's pack mule was tied.

"Didn't he have his reindeer?" Laura asked.

"You know he couldn't," Mary said. "There isn't any snow."

"Exactly," said Mr. Edwards. "Santa Claus travels with a pack mule in the southwest."

Santa Claus opened the pack and took out the presents for Mary and Laura.

"Oh, what are they?" Laura cried.

But Mary asked, "Then what did he do?"

Santa Claus shook hands with Mr. Edwards and swung up on his fine bay horse. He tucked his long, white whiskers under his bandanna and said, "So long, Edwards."

Then Santa Claus rode away on the Fort Dodge trail, whistling and leading his pack mule behind him.

Laura and Mary were silent thinking of that.

Then Ma said, "You may look now, girls."

Laura saw that something was shining bright in the top of her stocking. She squealed and jumped out of bed. So did Mary, but Laura beat her to the fireplace.

The shining thing was a glittering new tin cup. Mary had one exactly like it. Now they had tin cups of their very own.

Laura jumped up and down and

shouted and laughed. Mary stood still and looked with shining eyes at her own tin cup.

They plunged their hands into the stockings again. Out came two long sticks of candy. It was peppermint candy, striped red and white.

They looked and looked at the beautiful candy. Laura licked her stick, just one lick. But Mary was not so greedy. She didn't take even one lick.

And the stockings weren't empty yet! Mary and Laura reached in and pulled out two small packages. Inside each package was a little heart-shaped cake. The tops of the little cakes were sprinkled with white sugar. The sparkling grains looked like tiny drifts of snow.

The cakes were too pretty to eat. Mary and Laura just looked at them. But at last Laura turned hers over. She nibbled a tiny nibble from underneath, where it wouldn't show. The inside of the little cake was white, too!

Laura and Mary didn't think to look in their stockings again. The cups and the candy and the cakes were almost too much. They were too happy to speak. But then Ma asked if they were sure the stockings were empty.

Laura and Mary reached inside one more time. In the very toe of each stocking was a shining bright new penny!

Now they each had a penny of their very own. A cup and a cake and a stick of candy *and* a penny! There never had been such a Christmas.

Laura and Mary were so happy, they forgot about Mr. Edwards. They even forgot about Santa Claus.

In a minute, they would have re-membered. But before they did, Ma said gently, "Aren't you going to thank Mr. Edwards?"

"Oh, thank you, Mr. Edwards! Thank you!" Laura and Mary said. And they meant it with all their hearts.

Then Mr. Edwards stuck his hands into his pockets and took out nine sweet potatoes. He had brought them all the way from town. He thought Pa and Ma might like sweet potatoes with the Christmas turkey.

Now for Christmas dinner there was the big, juicy, roasted turkey. There were the soft, buttery sweet potatoes. And there was a fresh loaf of warm bread.

After all that there were dried black-berries and more little cakes. But these little cakes were made with brown sugar.

They did not have white sugar sprinkled over their tops.

After dinner, Pa and Ma and Mr. Edwards sat by the fire and talked.

Mary and Laura looked at their beautiful cakes and played with their pennies and drank water out of their new tin cups. Little by little, they licked their sticks of candy.

That was a happy Christmas.

CHAPTER 6

The Christmas Horses

Laura and Mary and baby Carrie and Ma and Pa spent the next Christmas in Minnesota. They had moved to a funny little house on the banks of Plum Creek. The house was called a dugout, and it was built right into the side of a hill. The walls were dirt. The floor was dirt. And the roof was grass that waved in the wind.

The dugout was snug and cozy, but there was no chimney. Laura and Mary knew that Santa Claus could not come without a chimney.

One day Mary asked Ma how Santa Claus would come.

Ma was ironing. She did not answer. Instead she asked, "What do you girls want for Christmas?"

"I want candy," Laura said.

"So do I," said Mary.

"And a new winter dress, and a coat, and a hood," said Mary.

"So do I," said Laura. "And a dress for Charlotte, and—"

"Do you know what Pa wants for Christmas?" Ma asked.

Laura and Mary did not know.

"Horses," Ma said. "Would you girls like that?"

Laura and Mary looked at each other.

"I only thought," Ma went on, "if we

all wished for horses, and nothing but horses, then maybe—"

Laura and Mary were quiet. They knew what Ma wanted them to do.

She wanted them to wish for nothing but horses for Pa. If they wished only for horses, that's what Santa would bring. No candy, no dresses, no new winter coats.

Laura felt funny. She knew that Pa needed new horses to help him on the

farm. But horses were everyday. They were not Christmas. It was hard to think of Santa Claus and horses at the same time.

Laura and Mary looked at each other again, then looked away. They did not say anything. Even Mary, who was always so good, did not say a word.

That night after supper, Pa drew Laura and Mary close to him in the crooks of his arms. Laura looked up at his face. Then she snuggled against him and said, "Pa."

"What is it, Half-Pint?" Pa asked.

"Pa, I want Santa Claus to bring—"

"What?" Pa asked.

"Horses," said Laura. "If you will let me ride them sometimes."

"So do I!" said Mary. But Laura was happy that she had said it first.

Pa was surprised. His eyes were soft

and bright. "Would you girls really like horses?" he asked.

"Oh yes, Pa!" they said.

"In that case," said Pa, smiling, "I have an idea that Santa Claus will bring us all a fine team of horses."

That settled it. They would not have any Christmas, only horses.

Laura felt glad almost right away. She thought of horses, sleek and shining. She could see their manes and tails blowing in the wind. She knew horses ran on swift feet and sniffed the air with velvety noses. Horses looked at everything with bright, soft eyes. And Pa would let her ride them. Laura fell asleep that night dreaming of horses.

CHAPTER 7

Horses and Candy

The next morning, snow was in the air. Hard bits of snow were leaping and whirling in the cold wind.

Laura and Mary could not go out to play. Even Pa stayed inside, mending his boots. Ma read from the story called *Millbank*.

Mary sewed, and Laura played with Charlotte.

That afternoon, when baby Carrie was asleep, Ma told them there would be one Christmas present after all. Mary and Laura could make a button string for Carrie!

Laura and Mary climbed onto their bed and turned their backs to Carrie. Ma brought them her button box.

The box was full of pretty buttons. Ma had saved buttons since she was smaller than Laura. And she had buttons that her mother had saved when her mother was a little girl.

The box was almost full. There were blue buttons and red buttons. Silver buttons and gold buttons. Shiny black glass buttons, painted china buttons, and striped buttons. There were buttons that looked like juicy blackberries. And there was even one tiny dog-head button. Laura squealed when she saw it.

"Shh!" Ma said. But Carrie did not wake up.

Ma gave them all those buttons to make a button string for Carrie.

Now Laura did not mind staying in the dugout. Outside, the cold wind made the tops of the trees rattle. Inside, Laura and Mary were warm and cozy. And they had a secret.

It was hard to keep Carrie from finding out. Every day Laura and Mary played with Carrie and gave her everything she wanted. They hugged her and sang to her. They tried to get her to sleep whenever they could. Then they worked on the button string.

Mary had one end of the string and Laura had the other. They picked out the buttons they wanted and strung them on the string. They held the string out to look at it. They took off some buttons and put on others.

Sometimes they took every button off and started all over again. They were

going to make the most beautiful button string in the world.

One morning Ma told them that they must finish the button string. It was the day before Christmas.

But they could not get Carrie to sleep. She ran and shouted. She skipped and sang. She did not get tired. Mary told her to sit still like a little lady, but she wouldn't.

Laura let her hold Charlotte. Carrie bounced Charlotte up and down and flung her against the wall.

Finally Ma took Carrie in her lap and sang to her in a sweet, low voice. Laura and Mary sat perfectly still. Lower and lower Ma sang. Carrie's eyes blinked till they shut. Quietly, Ma stopped singing.

Carrie's eyes popped open.

"More! More!" she shouted.

Ma sang another song. At last Carrie fell asleep.

As quickly as they could, Laura and Mary finished the button string. Ma tied the ends together, and it was done. It was a beautiful button string.

That evening after supper, when Carrie was sound asleep, Ma hung her clean little pair of stockings from the edge of the table. Laura and Mary slipped the button string into one stocking.

Then that was all. Mary and Laura began to climb into bed.

"Aren't you girls going to hang your stockings?" Pa asked.

"But I thought Santa Claus was going to bring us horses," Laura said.

"Maybe he will," said Pa. "But little girls always hang up their stockings on Christmas Eve, don't they?"

Laura did not know what to think. Neither did Mary. They had wished for nothing but horses, and they knew that horses would not fit into a stocking.

Ma took two clean stockings out of the clothes box. Pa helped hang them beside Carrie's. Laura and Mary said their prayers and went to bed, wondering.

In the morning Laura heard a fire crackling. She opened one eye a tiny bit.

In the lamplight she saw a bulge in her Christmas stocking. She yelled and jumped out of bed. Mary came running, too.

Inside Laura's stocking was a little paper package. Mary had one just like it.

The packages were filled with candy. Laura had six pieces and Mary had six. They had never seen such beautiful candy. It was too beautiful to eat.

Some pieces were like ribbons. Some were short and round with colored flowers in the middle. Some were perfectly round with stripes.

Carrie had candy too. In one of her stockings were four pieces of that beautiful candy.

In Carrie's other stocking was the button string. When Carrie saw it, her eyes and mouth grew round. She squealed and grabbed it and squealed again. She sat on

Pa's knee and looked at her candy and button string. She wriggled and laughed with joy.

Laura and Mary were glad they had worked so hard on the button string.

"Do you suppose there is anything for us in the stable?" Pa asked.

"Dress as fast as you can, girls," Ma said. "Go to the stable and see what Pa finds."

Laura and Mary put on their stockings and shoes. Ma wrapped their shawls under their chins. They ran out into the cold.

Pa stood waiting in the stable door. He laughed when he saw Laura and Mary.

Standing inside the stable were two horses. Their red-brown coats shone like silk. They had black manes and black tails. Their eyes were bright and gentle.

Laura held out her hand. The horses put their velvety noses down and nibbled softly at it. Their breath was warm.

"Well, Laura and Mary!" said Pa. "How do you girls like your Christmas?"

"Very much, Pa," said Mary.

But Laura could only say "Oh, Pa!"

"Who wants to ride the Christmas horses?" Pa asked. His eyes were shining.

Laura could hardly wait. Pa lifted Mary up first and showed her how to hold on to the mane. He told her not to be afraid.

Then Pa's strong arms swung Laura up into the air, and she was sitting on the other horse's big, gentle back.

Everything outside was glittering now. The sun was shining on the snow and frost.

Pa led the way down to the creek. The horses lifted their heads and took deep breaths. The cold whooshed out of their noses. Their velvety ears pricked forward, then back and forward again.

Laura held on to her horse's mane and laughed. Mary laughed too.

And then Pa's laugh rang out in the sparkling cold Christmas morning.

They were all so happy. Carrie had her button string—the most beautiful button string in the world. And Laura and Mary were riding the Christmas horses.

CHAPTER 8

Secrets and Surprises

A few years later, when winter came again, Pa was working for the railroad. Laura and Mary were getting to be big girls, and Carrie wasn't a baby anymore. Now they had a new little baby sister. Her name was Grace.

They were all living in a big wooden house near Silver Lake in Dakota Territory. The rooms of the house were full of Christmas secrets.

Mary was knitting new, warm socks for Pa. Laura was making him a necktie from a piece of silk she had found in Ma's scrap bag.

Together in the attic, Laura and Carrie were making an apron for Ma from an old calico curtain. And Mary was sewing Ma a fine white handkerchief.

When they were all finished, they put the handkerchief in the apron pocket. Then they wrapped the apron in tissue paper and hid it so Ma would not find it before Christmas.

Ma was helping Laura and Carrie make bed shoes for Mary. She took an old blanket that was worn out in the middle. She cut two pieces from the pretty red-and-green-striped ends.

Laura made one shoe and Carrie made the other. They trimmed the shoes with tassels of yarn and hid the shoes in Ma's bedroom.

Laura and Mary wanted to make mittens for Carrie, but they didn't have enough yarn. There was a little white yarn and a little red and a little blue.

"I know!" Mary said. "We'll make the hands white and the wrists in red and blue stripes."

Every morning while Carrie was making her bed in the attic, Laura and Mary knitted as fast as they could. When they heard her coming down the stairs, they hid the mittens in Mary's knitting basket.

Grace's Christmas present was going to be the prettiest of all. It was a little blue coat and hood. Laura and Carrie sewed the seams, and Mary put the tiny stitches in the hem. Ma made the hood.

They all worked on Grace's present

together by the fire. Grace was so little, she didn't notice.

"It's like making doll's clothes," Laura said.

"Grace will be prettier than any doll," Mary declared.

"Oh, let's put them on her now!" Carrie cried, dancing up and down.

But Ma said the coat and the hood must wait until Christmas morning.

The day before Christmas, it snowed and snowed. The flakes were soft and large.

When Pa came in from the stable, he stamped the snow from his feet. He broke the ice from his mustache.

"Whew!" he said. "It's too cold for Santa Claus to be out." His eyes twinkled when he looked at Carrie.

"We don't need Santa Claus! We've all been—" Carrie began, and then she clapped her hand over her mouth. She had almost told about the secrets.

At supper, they talked about other Christmases. They had had so many Christmases together. And here they were together again, warm and fed and happy.

Laura still had her precious Charlotte, the doll from her Christmas stocking in the Big Woods of Wisconsin. Laura and Mary remembered how Mr. Edwards had swum across the roaring creek to bring them their presents from Santa Claus. And they still had their beautiful Christmas horses.

Laura looked at Carrie.

"This is the best Christmas of all," she said. "Because now Carrie is old enough to know about Christmas, and now we have Grace."

Carrie smiled. Grace sat gurgling on

Ma's lap. Her hair was the color of sunshine, and her eyes were as blue as violets.

"Yes, this is the best Christmas after all," Mary said.

After supper, Pa went to get his fiddle, and they all sang,

> *"Jingle bells, jingle bells,*
> *Jingle all the way!*
> *Oh, what fun it is to ride,*
> *In a one-hoss open sleigh!"*

Through the music, Mary cried out, "What's that?"

"What, Mary?" Pa asked.

They all listened, and this time they all heard it. Out in the stormy night, a man shouted.

Pa laid the fiddle in its box and opened the door. The cold and the snow swirled in.

"Hullo-o-o, Ingalls," a voice shouted.

"It's Boast!" Pa cried. He put on his coat and cap and went outside.

Mr. Boast was going to be their new neighbor. He had gone away for the winter, and they hadn't expected him back until spring.

"He must be nearly frozen!" Ma cried. She hurried to put more coal on the fire.

When the door opened again, Pa called, "Here's Mrs. Boast too, Caroline!"

Mrs. Boast was a great bundle of coats and blankets. Ma helped her take off layer after layer, while Pa and Mr. Boast put the horses in the stable.

Mrs. Boast sat down beside Mary. She told them how their sled had gotten stuck in a snowdrift. They had had to go a long way in the freezing cold on horseback.

"We were so glad to see your light," Mrs. Boast said. "And when we heard your singing, you don't know how good it sounded."

Pa and Mr. Boast came in stamping snow from their boots. Mr. Boast's big laugh filled the whole house, and then everyone started laughing at once.

As the Boasts warmed themselves by the fire, Pa played a few more songs on his fiddle. Then everyone got ready for bed. Laura thought how jolly Christmas would be with their surprise guests.

Then she remembered all the Christmas secrets hidden in the house. There
were no presents for Mr. and Mrs. Boast!

CHAPTER 9

A Merry Christmas

When Laura woke up in the morning, she dressed quickly and hurried downstairs to help Ma get breakfast.

But Mrs. Boast was already there, helping Ma. The room was warm from the glowing stove, and the table was set.

"Merry Christmas!" Ma and Mrs. Boast said together.

"Merry Christmas," Laura answered.

Laura stared at the table. At each place there were packages.

Some were small and some were large. Some were wrapped in colored tissue paper and others were wrapped in plain brown paper tied with colored string.

"We didn't hang up stockings last night," said Ma. "So this is our Christmas breakfast table."

Laura went back upstairs. She told Mary and Carrie about the table with all the presents on it.

"Ma knew where we hid all the presents but hers," Laura said.

"But there isn't anything for Mr. and Mrs. Boast," Mary cried.

"Ma will fix it," Laura said.

"How can she?" Mary asked. "We didn't know they were coming!"

"Ma can fix anything," said Laura.

Laura took Ma's present from its hiding place. She held it behind her back as they all went downstairs. Quickly, she put the present on Ma's plate.

Laura saw that there was a little package on Mrs. Boast's plate, and another on Mr. Boast's.

"Mewy Cwismas! Mewy Cwismas!" Grace shouted. She wriggled out of Mary's arms and ran about, shouting.

Pa picked up Grace and tossed her in the air, just as he used to do to Laura when Laura was a little girl. Grace screamed with laughter.

Then they all sat down to open their presents and eat their breakfast.

Mrs. Boast opened her present first because she was company. Inside she found a handkerchief trimmed with lace. Laura saw that it was Ma's best Sunday handkerchief. Mrs. Boast was so surprised that there was a gift for her. She smiled happily and thanked them all.

Mr. Boast went next. His present was

 64

wristlets. They were knitted in stripes of red and gray. Laura knew that the wristlets had been for Pa. But Ma could knit some more after Christmas.

Pa said his new socks were just what he needed. And he liked the necktie that Laura had made.

"I'll put this on right after breakfast!" he said.

Then Ma unwrapped her pretty apron. She put it on at once and stood up for them all to see.

"There's more, Ma!" Carrie cried out. "Look in the pocket!"

Ma took out the handkerchief. She was so surprised. She looked at Laura and Mary and Carrie with shining eyes. To think that she had just given away her Sunday-best handkerchief, and now she had a brand-new one.

"Such a pretty handkerchief, too!"
Ma said.

Mary loved her soft, warm bed shoes.
Carrie put on her mittens and softly
clapped her hands.

"My Fourth of July mittens!" she said.
"Oh, see my Fourth of July mittens!"

Then Laura opened her package. It was
an apron just like Ma's! It was smaller than

Ma's, and it had two pockets instead of one. But it was made from the same calico.

All that time, Ma had been making an apron for Laura, and Laura had been making an apron for Ma—using the same old curtains!

Mary and Carrie had almost burst with the two secrets.

"Oh, thank you! Thank you all!" Laura said.

Then came the best part of all. Everyone watched while Ma wrapped Grace in her new coat and put the new hood over her golden hair.

Grace was so pretty and so happy, Laura could not look at her long enough.

There was still another package on Laura's plate. When she looked around, she saw that Mary and Carrie and Grace each had one too.

All at once, they unwrapped the packages. They each had a little pink bag full of candy.

"Christmas candy!" Laura and Mary and Carrie all cried at the same time.

It was beautiful candy. But they did not take one little bite. It was time to eat their Christmas breakfast.

Laura gathered up the paper wrappings. Then she helped Ma serve the food.

There were hot biscuits and fried potatoes and a bowl of thick gravy. Best of all, there was a glass dish full of applesauce.

Nothing could taste better than hot biscuits and applesauce. A breakfast like this came only once a year, just like Christmas.

After everyone had eaten, Pa and Mr. Boast went to get Mr. Boast's sled. Mary took Grace on her lap in the rocking chair.

Carrie made the beds and swept. Ma and Laura and Mrs. Boast put on their old aprons and washed the dishes.

With such jolly company, the morning seemed to go in a minute. Christmas dinner was almost ready when Pa and Mr. Boast came back with the sled. A big jackrabbit was browning in the oven. Potatoes were boiling. The coffeepot bubbled on the back of the stove. The house was full of good smells.

Laura spread out the clean white tablecloth. In the center of the table she set the glass sugar bowl and the glass pitcher full of cream. Carrie laid out the knives and forks. Laura set all the plates in a pile at Pa's place.

Quickly Laura and Ma took off their work aprons and tied on their Christmas aprons.

"Come!" said Ma. "Dinner is ready."

Pa heaped each plate with roast rabbit and stuffing and mashed potatoes and gravy. They all took big second helpings. Then Pa and Mr. Boast took big third helpings.

Pa was about to take another helping, but Ma told him to save some room.

"You don't mean there's more?" asked Pa.

Ma stepped into the pantry and brought out one more thing.

"Pie!" said Pa.

Slowly they each ate a piece of delicious apple pie.

"I've never eaten a better Christmas dinner," said Mr. Boast with a deep sigh.

Later, after the dishes had been put away and Pa and Mr. Boast were playing checkers, Mrs. Boast took Laura aside.

She held up a full paper bag.

"It's a surprise," she said. "It's popcorn! Mr. Boast doesn't know I brought it."

Quietly, Ma and Mrs. Boast heated the iron kettle and poured in a handful of the yellow corn. The little kernels began to crackle. Pa and Mr. Boast looked up.

"Popcorn!" Pa cried.

"Nell, you rascal," Mr. Boast said.

Mrs. Boast laughed. She and Ma dipped the snowy popcorn from the kettle into a milk pan. Laura salted it. They popped another kettleful until the milk pan could hold no more.

Laura loved the crispy, crackly, melting-soft corn.

They all sat by the fireplace eating and talking and laughing. Soon it would be chore time and suppertime and the time when Pa would play his fiddle. Another Christmas would be over.

Laura looked around at all the happy, smiling faces.

"Every Christmas is better than the Christmas before," she thought. "It must be because I'm growing up."